W9-CKH-990

First Facts™

Why in the World?

How Many Fish in the Sea?

A Book about Oceans

by Linda Tagliaferro

Consultant:
Sandra Mather, PhD
Professor Emerita, Department of Geology and Astronomy
West Chester University, West Chester, Pennsylvania

Capstone press®

Mankato, Minnesota

First Facts is published by Capstone Press,
151 Good Counsel Drive, P.O. Box 669, Mankato, Minnesota 56002.
www.capstonepress.com

Copyright © 2007 by Capstone Press. All rights reserved.
No part of this publication may be reproduced in whole or in part, or stored in a retrieval system,
or transmitted in any form or by any means, electronic, mechanical, photocopying, recording, or
otherwise, without written permission of the publisher.
For information regarding permission, write to Capstone Press,
151 Good Counsel Drive, P.O. Box 669, Dept. R, Mankato, Minnesota 56002.
Printed in the United States of America

Library of Congress Cataloging-in-Publication Data
Tagliaferro, Linda.
How many fish in the sea? : a book about oceans / by Linda Tagliaferro.
p. cm.—(First facts. Why in the world?)
Summary: "A brief description of oceans, including waves and currents, animals, plants,
and the ocean floor"—Provided by publisher.
Includes bibliographical references and index.
ISBN-13: 978-0-7368-6786-3 (hardcover)
ISBN-10: 0-7368-6786-4 (hardcover)
1. Marine organisms—Juvenile literature. 2. Ocean—Juvenile literature. I. Title. II. Series.
QH91.16.T34 2007
551.46—dc22   2006025651

Editorial Credits
Megan Schoeneberger, editor; Juliette Peters, set designer; Renée Doyle, book designer;
    Wanda Winch, photo researcher/photo editor

Photo Credits
Bruce Coleman Inc./FLAP/Dr. D. P. Wilson, 13 (left)
Digital Vision, 16 (bottom), 20
ExploreTheAbyss.com/Peter Batson, 15
Minden Pictures/Chris Newbert, 18; Flip Nicklin, 13 (right); Norbert Wu, 12
NASA/SeaWiFS Project/Goddard Space Flight Center and ORBIMAGE, 6
Peter Arnold/Paul Springett, 21
SeaPics.com/James D. Watt, cover (left); Rowan Byrne, 8–9
Shutterstock/Darlene Tompkins, cover (right); Frank Hatcher, 7; Lavigne Herve, 16 (top right);
    Norman Chan, 5; Summer, 16 (top left)

1 2 3 4 5 6 12 11 10 09 08 07

Table of Contents

Are Oceans the Same as Seas?

All the salty water in the oceans and seas really makes up just one big world ocean. But land splits the big ocean into five major parts. We call them the Pacific, Atlantic, Indian, Antarctic, and Arctic oceans. Each ocean has smaller parts called seas. Seas are mostly surrounded by land.

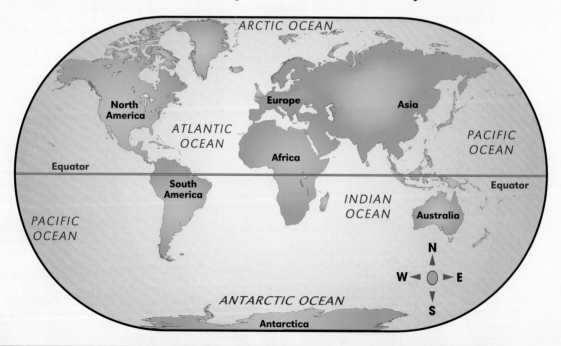

Scientific Inquiry

Asking questions and making observations like the ones in this book are how scientists begin their research. They follow a process known as scientific inquiry.

Ask a Question

Does the salt in ocean water help things float better than they would in freshwater?

Investigate

Pour 2 cups (480 mL) plain water into a small container. Then in another container, mix 2 cups (480 mL) warm water with 10 tablespoons (150 mL) salt and stir. Gently put a hard-boiled egg in the plain water. Does the egg float? Next, place the egg in salty water. What happens?

Explain

The egg sinks in plain water because it is more dense than the water. The egg floats in salt water because the added salt makes the water more dense than the egg. Record what you observe in your notebook and remember to keep asking questions.

Gulf Stream current

How Does the Water Move?

Steady winds make the ocean swirl in paths called **currents**. The currents flow like rivers, carrying water from one part of the ocean to another.

Wind also pushes ocean water into a wave. The first wave falls and sets off another. The second wave starts a third, and so on, until the wave crashes onto the beach.

What Does the Ocean Floor Look Like?

Near land, the ocean floor looks like a sandy beach. Going farther out, the ocean floor looks a lot like dry land. Wide, flat plains are broken up by tall mountains. Volcanoes ooze hot flowing lava. Deep **trenches** cut through the ocean bottom.

Sunlight Zone

Twilight Zone

Midnight Zone

Ocean Zones

How Deep Is the Ocean?

Very deep. Mariana Trench, the deepest point in the ocean, is deeper than Mount Everest is tall.

Ocean depths are split into zones. At the top, the **sunlight zone** gets lots of sunshine. Just below, the **twilight zone** gets little sunlight. The deep, dark **midnight zone** receives no sunlight.

Can Plants Grow in the Ocean?

Tons of plants drift near the ocean's surface. Plants grow only in the sunlight zone, where they can get the sunlight they need. Deeper water is too dark.

Some ocean plants, like **plankton**, can be too tiny to see. Others are giants. **Kelp** grows as tall as trees in ocean forests. Rootlike growths called holdfasts grip the ocean floor, so the plant is not carried away by waves.

plankton

Does Anything Live in the Midnight Zone?

Many strange creatures hang out in the midnight zone. These creatures need extra tricks to live in the dark, cold water. Some fish can even glow.

The anglerfish has a spine with a glowing tip. The tip hangs above its mouth like a fishing pole. Like bait, the light attracts other fish. The anglerfish then chomps down and swallows the fish.

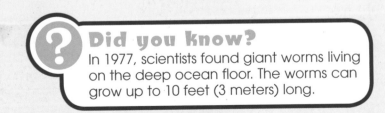

? Did you know?
In 1977, scientists found giant worms living on the deep ocean floor. The worms can grow up to 10 feet (3 meters) long.

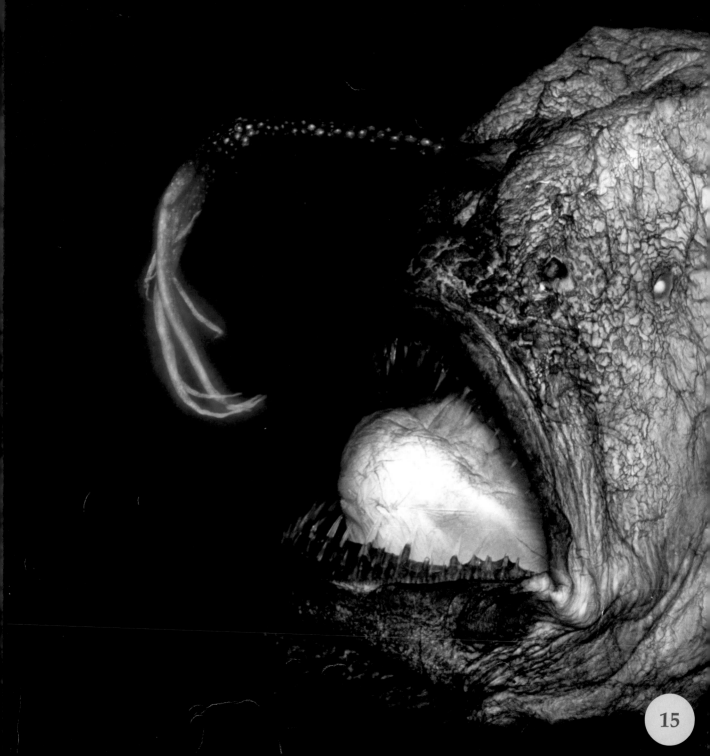

leafy sea dragon

octopus

white-tipped reef shark

What Other Creatures Live in the Ocean?

Dragons do, for one thing. Not the fire-breathing kind, but fish called sea dragons. They share the ocean with millions of other amazing animals. Octopuses glide along the bottom while sharks hunt other fish. Blue whales, the largest animals on earth, swim among tiny animals called plankton.

How Many Fish Are in the Ocean?

Too many to count! About 14,400 different kinds of fish swim in the ocean. And scientists are using underwater **vessels** and other tools to discover even more fish we have never seen before. What they learn can help us protect the big blue ocean and the many animals that swim, float, or paddle there.

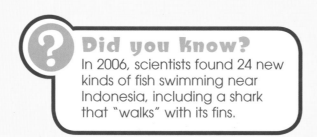

? Did you know?
In 2006, scientists found 24 new kinds of fish swimming near Indonesia, including a shark that "walks" with its fins.

Coral reefs look like underwater gardens of colorful plants and rocks. But corals aren't plants or rocks. They're animals with skeletons outside of their bodies. As corals die, new ones live on top of the old skeletons. After many years, layers of skeletons form a coral reef.

20

? Imagine being able to explore the ocean for months or even years at a time. But people can't stay underwater for very long without air to breathe. Think about how fish and other animals survive in the ocean. What would you need to be able to live in the ocean?

21

GLOSSARY

current (KUR-uhnt)—the movement of water in the ocean

kelp (KELP)—a large seaweed

midnight zone (MID-nite ZOHN)—the deep ocean layer where no light can reach

plankton (PLANGK-tuhn)—tiny plants and animals that drift or float in water

sunlight zone (SUHN-lite ZOHN)—the top layer of oceans; this zone receives enough sunlight for plants to grow.

trench (TRENCH)—a long, narrow valley along the ocean floor

twilight zone (TWYE-liyte ZOHN)—the middle ocean layer where some light can reach, but not enough for plants to grow

vessel (VESS-uhl)—a boat or a ship

READ MORE

Howard, Fran. *Oceans.* Habitats. Edina, Minn.: Abdo, 2006.

Royston, Angela. *Oceans.* My World of Geography. Chicago: Heinemann Library, 2005.

Sandler, Michael. *Oceans: Surviving in the Deep Sea.* X-treme Places. New York: Bearport, 2006.

INTERNET SITES

FactHound offers a safe, fun way to find Internet sites related to this book. All of the sites on FactHound have been researched by our staff.

Here's how:

1. Visit *www.facthound.com*

2. Choose your grade level.

3. Type in this book ID **0736867864** for age-appropriate sites. You may also browse subjects by clicking on letters, or by clicking on pictures and words.

4. Click on the **Fetch It** button.

FactHound will fetch the best sites for you!

INDEX